FIRST POEMS

illustrated by

BRENDA MEREDITH SEYMOUR

The Lutterworth Press

First published 1968

This impression 1991

The Publishers wish to make acknowledgement to the following for permission to include poems of which they control the copyright: The Literary Trustees of Walter de la Mare and The Society of Authors as their representative for "Someone"; David Higham Associates for "Waves" and "The Night Will Never Stay" (Copyright, 1951 by Eleanor Farjeon) and in the U.S.A., J. B. Lippincott Company; Mrs. H. M. Davies for "Leisure" from *The Complete Poems of W. H. Davies* (Copyright © 1963 by Jonathan Cape Ltd.) and in the U.S.A. by permission of Wesleyan University Press; Mr. Robert Graves, A. P. Watt & Son, and in the U.S.A. Collins-Knowlton-Wing Inc. for "I'd Love to be a Fairy's Child"; and to the Bodleian Library (Oxford), Methuen & Co. Ltd., and Charles Scribner's Sons in the U.S.A. and Canada for "Ducks' Ditty" from *The Wind in the Willows* by Kenneth Grahame.

Printed in Hong Kong by Colorcraft Ltd

CONTENTS

SPRING

Sound the flute!
Now 'tis mute;
Birds delight
Day and night
Nightingale
In the dale;
Lark in the sky
Merrily,
Merrily, merrily to welcome
                in the year.

4

Little boy,
Full of joy;
Little girl,
Sweet and small;
Cock does crow,
So do you;
Merry voice
Infant noise;
Merrily, merrily to welcome
in the year.

Little lamb,
Here I am;
Let me pull
Your soft wool;
Let me kiss
Your soft face;
Merrily, merrily we welcome
                in the year.

William Blake

SNOWDROPS

I like to think
That, long ago,
There fell to earth
Some flakes of snow
Which loved this cold,
Grey world of ours
So much, they stayed
As snowdrop flowers.

Mary Vivian

SPRING

Now daisies pied, and violets blue,
And lady-smocks all silver white,
And cuckoo-buds of yellow hue
Do paint the meadows with delight,
The cuckoo now on every tree
Sings cuckoo, cuckoo.

William Shakespeare

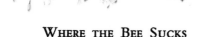

WHERE THE BEE SUCKS

Where the bee sucks, there suck I;
In a cowslip's bell I lie;
There I couch when owls do cry.
On the bat's back I do fly
After summer merrily.
Merrily, merrily shall I live now
Under the blossom that hangs on
                  the bough.

William Shakespeare

THE LAMB

Little lamb, who made thee?
Dost thou know who made thee,
Gave thee life and bade thee feed
By the stream and o'er the mead.
Gave thee clothing of delight,
Softest clothing, woolly, bright;
Gave thee such a tender voice,
Making all the vales rejoice?
Little lamb, who made thee?
Dost thou know who made thee?

Little lamb, I'll tell thee;
Little lamb, I'll tell thee:
He is called by thy name,
For He calls Himself a Lamb;
He is meek, and He is mild,
He became a little child.
I a child, and thou a lamb,
We are called by His name.
Little lamb, God bless thee!
Little lamb, God bless thee!

William Blake

SOMEONE

Someone came knocking
At my wee small door;
Someone came knocking,
I'm sure – sure – sure;
I listened, I opened,
I looked to left and right,
But nought there was a-stirring
In the still dark night.

Only the busy beetle
Tap-tapping in the wall,
Only from the forest
The screech-owl's call,
Only the cricket whistling
While the dewdrops fall,
So I know not who came knocking,
At all, at all, at all.

Walter de la Mare

WINDY NIGHTS

Whenever the moon and stars are set,
Whenever the wind is high,
All night long in the dark and wet,
A man goes riding by.
Late in the night when the fires are out,
Why does he gallop and gallop about?

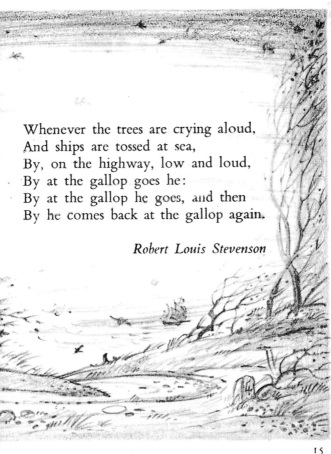

Whenever the trees are crying aloud,
And ships are tossed at sea,
By, on the highway, low and loud,
By at the gallop goes he:
By at the gallop he goes, and then
By he comes back at the gallop again.

Robert Louis Stevenson

DUCKS' DITTY

All along the backwater,
Through the rushes tall,
Ducks are a-dabbling,
Up tails all!

Ducks' tails, drakes' tails,
Yellow feet a-quiver,
Yellow bills all out of sight
Busy in the river!

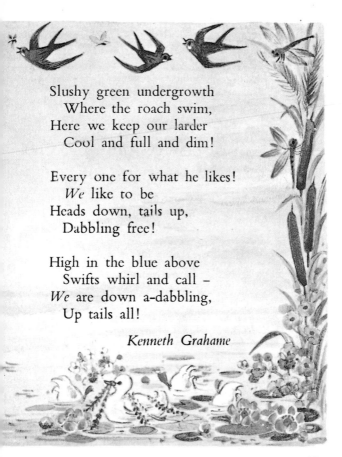

Slushy green undergrowth
  Where the roach swim,
Here we keep our larder
  Cool and full and dim!

Every one for what he likes!
  We like to be
Heads down, tails up,
  Dabbling free!

High in the blue above
  Swifts whirl and call –
We are down a-dabbling,
  Up tails all!

          Kenneth Grahame

LEISURE

What is this life if, full of care,
We have no time to stand and stare?

No time to stand beneath the boughs
And stare as long as sheep or cows.

No time to see, when woods we pass,
Where squirrels hide their nuts in grass.

No time to see, in broad daylight,
Streams full of stars, like skies at night.

No time to turn at Beauty's glance,
And watch her feet, how they can dance.

No time to wait till her mouth can
Enrich that smile her eyes began.

A poor life this if, full of care,
We have no time to stand and stare.

W. H. Davies

A Child's Thought

At seven, when I go to bed,
I find such pictures in my head:
Castles with dragons prowling round,
Gardens where magic fruits are found;
Fair ladies prisoned in a tower,
Or lost in an enchanted bower;
While gallant horsemen ride by streams
That border all this land of dreams
I find, so clearly in my head
At seven, when I go to bed.

At seven, when I wake again,
The magic land I seek in vain;
A chair stands where the castle frowned;
The carpet hides the garden ground,
No fairies trip across the floor,
Boots, and not horsemen, flank the door,
And where the blue streams rippling ran
Is now a bath and water-can;
I seek the magic land in vain
At seven, when I wake again.

Robert Louis Stevenson

A Knight came riding

A knight came riding from the East,
   Jennifer, gentle and rosemarie,
Who had been wooing at many a place,
   As the dove flies over the mulberry tree.
He came and knocked at the lady's gate,
One evening when it was growing late.
The eldest sister let him in,
And pinned the door with a silver pin.
The second sister, she made his bed
And laid soft pillows under his head.
The youngest sister was bold and bright
And she would wed with this unco'
               knight.

"If you will answer me questions three,
This very day will I marry thee.

"O what is louder nor a horn?
And what is sharper nor a thorn?
"What is heavier nor the lead?
And what is better nor the bread?
"O what is higher nor the tree?
And what is deeper nor the sea?"
"O, shame is louder nor a horn,
And hunger is sharper nor a thorn.
"And sin is heavier nor the lead,
And the blessing's better nor the bread.
"O, Heaven is higher nor the tree,
And love is deeper nor the sea."
"O, you have answered my questions
  Jennifer, gentle and rosemarie, [three,
And so, fair maid, I'll marry with thee,
  As the dove flies over the mulberry tree."

Anon

THERE ARE BIG WAVES

There are big waves and little waves,
  Green waves and blue,
Waves you can jump over,
  Waves you dive thro',
Waves that rise up
  Like a great water wall,
Waves that swell softly
  And don't break at all,
Waves that can whisper
  Waves that can roar,
And tiny waves that run at you
  Running on the shore.

Eleanor Farjeon

BOATS SAIL ON THE RIVERS

Boats sail on the rivers,
  And ships sail on the seas;
But clouds that sail across the sky
  Are prettier far than these.

There are bridges on the rivers,
  As pretty as you please;
But the bow that bridges heaven,
  And overtops the trees,
And builds a road from earth to sky,
  Is prettier far than these.

Christina Rossetti

THE THRUSH'S NEST

Within a thick and spreading hawthorn
                   bush,
That overhung a mole-hill large and
                   round,
I heard from morn to morn a merry
                   thrush
Sing hymns to sunrise, and I drank
                the sound
With joy; and, often an intruding guest,
I watched her secret toils from day
                to day –
How true she warped the moss to form
                a nest,
And modelled it within with wood
                and clay;

And by and by, like heath-bells gilt
                        with dew,
There lay her shining eggs, as bright
                        as flowers,
Ink-spotted over shells of greeny blue;
And there I witnessed, in the sunny hours
A brood of nature's minstrels chirp
                        and fly,
Glad as that sunshine and the laughing
                        sky.

John Clare

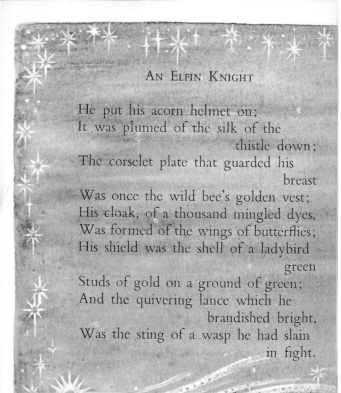

AN ELFIN KNIGHT

He put his acorn helmet on;
It was plumed of the silk of the
                       thistle down;
The corselet plate that guarded his
                           breast
Was once the wild bee's golden vest;
His cloak, of a thousand mingled dyes,
Was formed of the wings of butterflies;
His shield was the shell of a ladybird
                         green
Studs of gold on a ground of green;
And the quivering lance which he
                   brandished bright,
Was the sting of a wasp he had slain
                       in fight.

Swift he bestrode his firefly steed;
He bared his blade of the bent-grass blue;
He drove his spurs of the cockle-seed,
And away like a glance of thought
                        he flew,
To skim the heavens, and follow far
The fiery trail of the rocket star.

John Rodman Drake

THE KITTEN AT PLAY

See the kitten on the wall,
Sporting with the leaves that fall,
Withered leaves, one, two and three,
Falling from the elder-tree;
Through the calm and frosty air
Of the morning bright and fair.

See the kitten, how she starts,
Crouches, stretches, paws and darts;
With a tiger-leap half way
Now she meets her coming prey.
Lets it go as fast as then
Has it in her power again.

Now she works with three and four,
Like an Indian conjurer;
Quick as he in feats of art,
Gracefully she plays her part;
Yet were gazing thousands there,
What would little Tabby care?

William Wordsworth

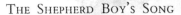

The Shepherd Boy's Song

He that is down needs fear no fall,
  He that is low, no pride;
He that is humble ever shall
  Have God to be his guide.

I am content with what I have,
  Little be it or much:
And, Lord, contentment still I crave,
  Because Thou savest such.

Fullness to such a burden is
  That go on pilgrimage:
Here little, and hereafter bliss,
  Is best from age to age.

John Bunyan

I'd love to be a Fairy's Child

Children born of fairy stock
Never need for shirt or frock,
Never want for food or fire,
Always get their heart's desire:
Jingle pockets full of gold,
Marry when they're seven years old,
Every fairy child may keep
Two strong ponies and ten sheep;
All have houses, each his own,
Built of brick or granite stone;
They live on cherries, they run wild –
I'd love to be a fairy's child.

Robert Graves

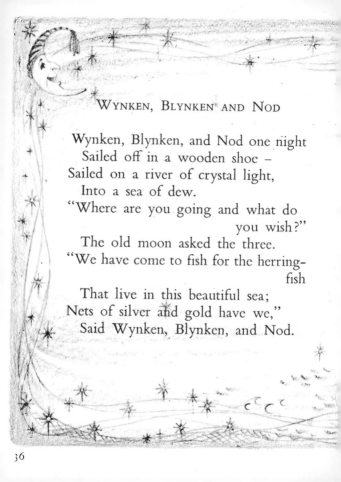

WYNKEN, BLYNKEN AND NOD

Wynken, Blynken, and Nod one night
   Sailed off in a wooden shoe –
Sailed on a river of crystal light,
   Into a sea of dew.
"Where are you going and what do
              you wish?"
   The old moon asked the three.
"We have come to fish for the herring-
              fish
   That live in this beautiful sea;
Nets of silver and gold have we,"
   Said Wynken, Blynken, and Nod.

The old moon laughed and sang a song,
   As they rocked in the wooden shoe,
And the wind that sped them all night
               long
   Ruffled the waves of dew.
The little stars were the herring-fish
   That lived in that beautiful sea –
"Now cast your nets wherever you
              wish –
   But never afeared are we";
So cried the stars to the fishermen three:
   Wynken, Blynken, and Nod.

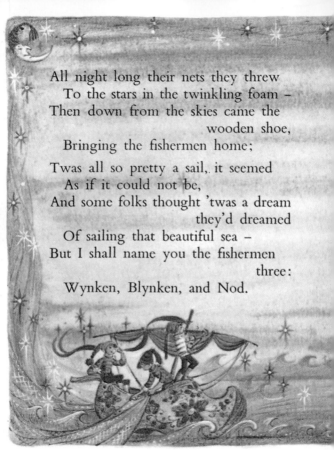

All night long their nets they threw
  To the stars in the twinkling foam –
Then down from the skies came the
                    wooden shoe,
  Bringing the fishermen home;

'Twas all so pretty a sail, it seemed
  As if it could not be,
And some folks thought 'twas a dream
                    they'd dreamed
  Of sailing that beautiful sea –
But I shall name you the fishermen
                    three:

  Wynken, Blynken, and Nod.

Wynken and Blynken are two little eyes,
　And Nod is a little head,
And the wooden shoe that sailed the
　　　　　　　　　　　skies
　Is a wee one's trundle-bed.
So shut your eyes while mother sings
　Of wonderful sights that be,
And you shall see the beautiful things
　As you rock on the misty sea,
Where the old shoe rocked the fishermen
　　　　　　　　　　　three:
　Wynken, Blynken, and Nod.

Eugene Field

THE NIGHT WILL NEVER STAY

The night will never stay,
  The night will still go by,
Though with a million stars
  You pin it to the sky,
Though you bind it with the blowing
                              wind
  And buckle it with the moon,
The night will slip away
  Like sorrow or a tune.

Eleanor Farjeon